My Daddy and Me

bookoli

I love my daddy
because in each photograph,

He does something silly
to make us all laugh!

I love my daddy
because he loves to play.
There's no braver knight
with dragons to slay!

I love my daddy
because when I feel blue,

He just seems to know
exactly what to do.

I love my daddy
because he likes to cook.

(Though he never follows
the recipes in the book!)

I love my daddy

because he'll zoom down the slide,

Push us on swings,

and give me a shoulder ride.

I love my daddy
because he can chase a firefly,
Then talk about the moon
and all the planets in the sky.

When we wish upon stars,
that our dreams will come true,
He says, "Who needs wishes?
When I've got you and you and you!"

I love my daddy
because if I scrape my knee,

He's ready with a kiss and a cuddle for me!

I love my daddy because when I'm scared at night,

He makes me feels safe and wraps me up tight.

We talk about shadows and how they are made.

Thanks to my daddy, I'm no longer afraid!

I love my daddy because he loves to nap.

And there's no place cozier, than snuggled on his lap.

I love my daddy
because he's so sweet.

He's thoughtful and kind,

to everyone we meet.

He teaches us to share
when we have something to lend.

It makes you feel good,
and you might make a friend!

I love my daddy
because I don't need a prize,

To know that he's proud,

I can see it in his eyes.

I love my daddy,
there's nothing he can't do.

And the best thing about him,
is that he loves me too!